The Shoe Shop Bears

The
Shoe Shop Bears

BY MARGARET J. BAKER

Illustrated by
C. WALTER HODGES

ARIEL BOOKS
FARRAR, STRAUS & GIROUX | NEW YORK

Contents

The Shoe Shop Bears

by MARGARET J. BAKER

illustrated by C. WALTER HODGES

Boots, Slippers, and Socks were three teddy
bears kept in a shoe shop to amuse young
customers, and everything in this delight-
ful story is seen through their eyes: the
nice old proprietor, Mr. Shoehorn, who
began to find the work too much for him;
his unimaginative successor, Mr. Wade;
the young assistant, Polly, eager and kind;
and the cats who visited the shop at night
through the skylight and brought all the
news of the town.

The bears were made so unhappy by Mr.
Wade that they determined to look for a
home of their own and thought they saw
the perfect opportunity for escape when
Christmas gifts were being collected to
hang on the big spruce outside the cathedral. But though they climbed into a box
of slippers and were hung on the tree, the
bears were sent back to the shoe shop.
Still, if it hadn't been for this escapade,
they would never have met Mr. Chesterfield, who was the comfort of the bishop's
childhood, nor have known about a friend-

ship between child and bear such as they
were longing for.

In a wonderful Christmas climax Polly
finds a way to make the bears' wish come
true.

The Shoe Shop Bears

Bears in Business

THE THREE teddy bears had been in Mr. Shoehorn's shoe shop in Cordwainer's Row for as long as most of the inhabitants of Slumber Lightly could remember. In the cathedral town, Wellington Boots, Slippers, and Socks were the only bears to be gainfully employed. They were proud to be in business.

Mr. Shoehorn's shop was in a narrow alleyway near the cathedral and the Bishop's palace. Next door to the

9

shoe shop was an old-established family grocer's. On the other side was a shop which sold church fittings: crimson hassocks with flaps like ears, carved hymn-boards, offertory bags, and brass candlesticks. The shops jostled together like nuts pressed between nutcrackers. Cordwainer's Row was so narrow it was a one-way street. But on blowing March mornings, in the distance at the end of the street, daffodils flowered on the smooth grass before the cathedral, and from the yard at the back of the shoe shop the Bishop's washing could be seen tossing on the line in the palace garden.

Cordwainer's Row was always busy. Clergymen hurried past the shops with their black cassocks blowing like the plumage of the jackdaws who built their nests among the worn stone carvings on the cathedral tower. Bright-cheeked choristers called at the shoe shop to choose their new football boots, and country house-wives paused to admire Mr. Shoehorn's new spring shoes. The leathers of his walking-shoes glowed like autumn leaves, and no shoes in all the town fitted so perfectly.

Mr. Shoehorn's shop itself looked like a highly polished and well-worn shoe. The step was hollowed by generations of customers, and the handle on the door glowed like dark amber barley-sugar. When the shop door was opened a bell rang, and Mr. Shoehorn came forward with a smile to serve his customer. The smile seemed to light up the whole interior of the small shop. It showed in every wrinkle of the old shopkeeper's face and sparkled from his gold-rimmed spectacles as well.

The three bears who sat in a battered basket-chair in

the children's part of the shop had no proper names. On the stock-list Mr. Shoehorn described them as *Three stuffed toy bears, large, medium, and small, for the comfort, amusement, and edification of juvenile customers during the fitting of their footwear.*

Wellington Boots had seen the whole description in the red-bound ledger, written in Mr. Shoehorn's flowing, copperplate hand. The bears were proud of the description. None of them knew exactly what "edification" meant, but it sounded as dignified as the pealing of the cathedral bells themselves. Mr. Shoehorn liked to say everything in threes. Anyone else might have had just two bears in his shop, but Mr. Shoehorn preferred to have three. The bears had chosen their own names from those they had seen printed on boxes in the shop.

Wellington Boots was the largest bear. He was only a little smaller than the youngest customers who came to the shop. Boots's fur was golden. The pads on his paws were made of real chamois leather, and his eyes were bright amber and black. Once Boots had possessed a growl, which sounded when he was hugged. Wellington Boots was a bear who was hugged a great deal, and the growl had soon worn itself out.

Boots was dependable and cheerful, even on wet Monday mornings. He knew more about shoes than any of the other bears. Boots knew that shoemakers had once been called cordwainers because they used leather which came from Cordova, in Spain. Boots knew the difference between an Oxford shoe and a Derby, and what a gentleman called Pfitzner had said about the little toe having only two joints. When a young woman

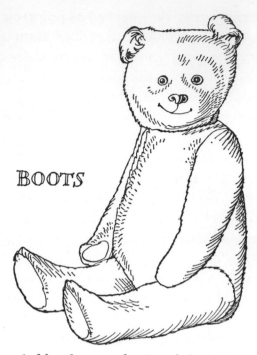

BOOTS

sat surrounded by dozens of pairs of shoes Boots, watching her with his head on one side, could always guess which shoes she would choose in the end.

"More than likely it will be the pair she tried on first," he would tell the others when they marveled at his guesswork, "but, all the same, a good shopkeeper doesn't rush it. It's best to let them waver till they settle for themselves. That's the long way around, but if you let them take it everyone will be happy, and there will be no regrets."

Slippers was the medium-sized bear. Her fur was worn smooth and short like honey-colored velvet. Her arms were thin because the sawdust had leaked out, and her paws were mended with pieces cut from a yellow

duster. Her eyes were made from black boot-buttons.
Even the most timid little girls from outlying hamlets,
visiting the town for the first time to buy their first pair
of walking-shoes, were comforted when they saw
Slippers and held her in their arms. Slippers wasn't really
beautiful any more, but children loved her just the same.
She was a kind bear. Her beauty was deep inside. However much sawdust leaked from her seams, nothing
could spoil it.

Slippers was timid herself. She worried a lot, and a
frown wrinkled the fur between her eyes. She worried
about Boots, whose hair was thinning on his muzzle
so that the canvas showed through. She worried about

SLIPPERS —

Socks, who sometimes took dangerous risks, especially with the dogs who often accompanied their owners into the shop. But Slippers worried most of all about moths. Moths scared her so much she never said the word except in a hushed whisper. Slippers always smelled of mothballs. She collected the mothballs from the boxes of lamb's-wool-lined boots when they were brought out of storage in the autumn. Exactly what harm moths did to bears Slippers would never say.

"If it's just making us go bald I won't bother," Socks protested between sneezes, as Slippers sprinkled him with powdered mothballs. "Mr. Shoehorn's almost bald himself, and he doesn't mind a bit."

Slippers only looked grave and took no notice. What moths could do to a toy bear had happened to one of her own relations, when he was packed away in a toy-cupboard. Afterwards the bear had never been seen again, and Slippers intended to take no chances.

Socks was the smallest bear. He had bright ginger fur and small glass eyes. Mr. Shoehorn had won the bear at a shooting-gallery on the pier when, as a cathedral sides-man,* he had accompanied the choir on their annual outing. The Bishop had won a vase painted with cupids and red roses. The vase still stood in a place of honor in his study below the blue-bladed oar he had used in the boat race many years before. Mr. Shoehorn's score, however, had been the highest of the whole party.

"Any prize he could have chosen," Socks often told the others, "a plaster Alsatian, *The Boyhood of Raleigh*,

* assistant to the lay honorary parish official called the churchwarden

SOCKS

in a real gilt frame, or a cut-glass jam dish with a silver-plated lid, but he chose me."

The small bear had taken his name from a box of men's socks. These were a discontinued line, but Socks didn't care. He was always in and out of trouble. His fur bore the stains of many of his investigations. Socks would try anything once, and, as Boots observed, that was usually once too often.

Boots enjoyed instructing the other bears in their duties. Perched on one of the mahogany fitting-stools, with a yellow pencil stuck behind his ear, Boots talked about their responsibilities.

"Our foremost task is to sit with the young customer

throughout the fitting of his or her shoes," he said. "So long as the child remains on these premises we are bound to fulfill a brief, but nevertheless not unimportant, role. For the time being we stand *in loco parentis*."

"But doesn't that mean in place of their parents?" asked Slippers. "Usually they come with their mother at least."

Boots swallowed hard, and frowned. It was a tag of Latin he had found in the back of an old dictionary kept in the cash-desk, and he had been saving it to use on the first possible occasion.

"And we don't usually stand," added Socks. "That's all right for you because with big pads you can balance, but Slippers and I find it better to sit."

"Sitting or standing, we replace the comfort of the teddy bears the children have left at home," said Boots patiently. "It is a humble yet honored position for us to fill, and, whatever the obstacles or difficulties we may encounter, we must rise above them and do our duty." Boots bent his head to stare severely at the youngest bear. He was the only one among them who could swivel his head downward as well as turn it from side to side. Boots enjoyed doing it even if the pencil toppled from behind his ear and rolled away across the floor.

"What about boys with chewing gum?" asked Socks. "And the Bishop's grand-niece, who threw Slippers right over the counter because her mother wouldn't buy her those red dancing-shoes?"

"That was quite understandable," said Slippers. "She's simply a child who knows her own mind. Mr. Shoehorn had a charming letter of apology afterwards, in which she sent me her special love. It was all done in capitals on pink notepaper with roses in the corner and sealed with red wax. To my mind, dogs are a far greater difficulty. A poodle had Socks in his mouth only last week, and he's dribbled sawdust ever since."

Boots raised his head and stood up very straight, so that the fine curve of his chest showed to its best. His eyes shone in the dim light of a street lamp, which, after closing-time, was the only light in the shop.

"Whatever the problems or indignities," he said, "in trade we must always remember that the customer is always right. It is not for us to criticize or question. We are simply small cog-wheels in a big machine. The smooth running of that machine depends on all and every one of us, however humble." He frowned hard at Socks, who giggled and slid backward down one of the footrests.

"Of course you are right, Boots dear," said Slippers, who had thought he had been a shade put out by her correction of the Latin tag. "No bear in trade could have done more than you. Mr. Shoehorn's said again and again that you're the best assistant he's ever had, and I'm sure he really means it."

Slippers put her paw through the arm of the larger bear, and he patted it. She rested her head against his broad chest and pressed a powdered mothball quietly into a patch of fur on his shoulders which seemed to be rather thin, so that he sneezed but never noticed what she had done.

After dark, when the CLOSED sign hung in the glass-topped door, the shoe shop belonged to the bears alone.

17

A fire still glowed in the hob-grate, and the bears sat around it resting, with their day's work done. It was then that Wellington Boots studied old shoe catalogs with pictures of Balmoral boots, ladies' spats and leather gaiters, and nodded over the books on the making of boots and shoes which the old shopkeeper always kept at hand.

"We should know our trade," Boots often told the others, as he puzzled over a diagram of the human foot or the correct way to waterproof a pair of hunting-boots.

While Boots read, the other bears played hide-and-seek around the shop. Sometimes they all danced before the low mirrors in which the customers inspected their new shoes. After their games they tidied the shop. Slippers made them polish every paw-mark from the linoleum and brush up every ginger hair from the Turkey carpet. In the morning, when Mr. Shoehorn arrived to open the shop, there was never a fitting-stool out of line or a shoe-box out of place.

The bears enjoyed most the nights when they had company. Their friends were three cats who also had jobs in the town. Hobson, a large black-and-white cat, worked in the grocer's next door. He sat on his own chair by the bacon counter, just out of reach of the bacon slicer, yet handy to receive any trimmings from the assistant in charge. Occasionally newcomers to the town pushed Hobson off his chair so that they might set down their shopping-baskets. When this happened Hobson simply stared at the offenders with his large green eyes, and they seldom did it twice. Hobson knew as much about the grocery trade as Boots knew about shoes. Anyone who was a friend of Hobson's received the finest butter, the mildest bacon, and the most tasty cheese, for the man in charge of the bacon counter respected Hobson's judgment of people and cheese.

Hobson was usually accompanied by Big Tom and Little Tom from the cathedral. The two lean black cats patrolled the aisles by day and night, watchful for the slightest sign of a mouse. The appointment of cathedral-mousers had always been in their family. It had been handed down from father to son for hundreds of years.

The cats entered the shop by a skylight in the cloak-room at the rear of the shop. Mr. Shoehorn left it open on purpose so that Hobson could look in from time to time and keep the premises free of mice.

The cats brought the bears all the news of the town. Hobson heard a great deal of gossip as he sat, apparently more than half asleep, on his chair in the shop. Big Tom and Little Tom picked up the rest. They spent all their free time stalking along the city roofs, and were acquainted with every other cat in the city. They knew every pinnacle and flying-buttress of the cathedral itself. As they padded around the moonlit cathedral during their working hours, the aisles with their soaring pillars might have been woodland pathways, and when dawn broke the great eastern window glittered like a jungle flower.

"I wish we could go out like the cats," Socks remarked, after one of their visits. "Dozens of bears do.

19

I've often seen them ride by in prams or perched in the back window of a car. That way would be the best of all."

"Shop bears must be prepared to give up the more domestic pleasures," Boots told him firmly. Yet the big bear knew they were all sad when, with the purchase completed, a young customer had to bid them good-bye.

Once a little girl, who had come to the shop for her first pair of lace-up brown-calf shoes, had taken Slippers away with her, clutched in her arms. Halfway down

Cordwainer's Row, her mother had noticed what she had done. When they returned with the bear Mr. Shoehorn had offered to let the little girl keep it, but her mother had insisted that Slippers be given back.

But all the bears were so interested in their work, and so fond of the old shopkeeper, that on the whole they were happy and content. Every night, when the fire in the hob-grate had died to a heap of ash, the policeman who patrolled Cordwainer's Row paused outside the shop to try the lock and make sure all was well. When he shone his flashlight through the glass-topped door he always saw the bears huddled close together in their basket-chair beside the showcase of children's shoes. The three bears slept so soundly and were so still that it was impossible to imagine they had ever stirred.

Under New Management

EVERY DAY when Mr. Shoehorn opened the shop on the stroke of nine, the bears forgot all their troubles. While Mr. Shoehorn polished the shoes to set in the window, with the best carnauba wax made from the leaves of Brazilian palm-trees, he talked to the three bears about the day's work, just as if they were his most valued assistants.

"Now, let's see, today the Bishop's little grand-niece will be in for her sandal that had the broken strap," he told the bears, as they sat alert in their basket-chair beside the showcase full of buckle slippers, red-barred walking-shoes, and buckskin sandals. "The Bishop will be in himself, just before Evensong, for his new gaiters. Mrs. Saltmarsh's brogues were invoiced yesterday and should be on the station van.* Colonel Flintlock's boots have been waterproofed with cod-liver oil and tallow, just as he wished, and his wife will collect them. She's bringing along her granddaughter for a pair of lace-up

* railway baggage car

calf-leather shoes. Size two it will be, most likely. We'll have three fittings ready and Slippers handy to see that all goes without a hitch. Her mother was a timid little thing, and subject to the worst chilblains I have known."

Mr. Shoehorn never seemed to mind that the bears couldn't reply. As Boots always told them, bears were meant to be seen and not heard.

The bears first guessed something was wrong when, in December, on a Monday morning, Mr. Shoehorn failed to open the shop. All that week the CLOSED sign hung on the shop door. When Mr. Shoehorn returned the following Monday, he looked tired and ill.

"Is it moths?" Socks whispered. "Like your relation in the toy-cupboard, who was never seen again?"

"Of course not," said Slippers shortly. "What's bad for bears isn't the same for people. You should know that."

But they left two mothballs in Mr. Shoehorn's overcoat pocket just in case, and hoped for the best. The old shopkeeper was well enough to arrange the January sale, but his sparse hair looked whiter and his dark suit seemed suddenly much too large. When fitting a pair of shoes, he took longer to rise to his feet and climb the ladder to fetch another size from an upper shelf.

When they called at night, the cats were full of rumors.

"The doctor told him he should retire," said Big Tom.

"We heard from the ginger cat who belongs to the nurse who helps him," said Little Tom.

"There's nothing fundamentally wrong, but he needs

a rest," Big Tom added. "Otherwise the doctor wouldn't answer for the consequences!"

Hobson used much shorter words than the cathedral cats, and the bears found him less alarming.

"Your old master is just too old to work any more. He'll have to retire, like the man who was on the bacon counter when I went there first as a kitten. He has a cottage in the country now and grows prize tomatoes."

"But what will happen to us and the shop?" Slippers asked.

Hobson considered, with his white chin sunk on his folded black paws.

"Since the shop does good business, it's sure to be kept as a shoe shop and sold as a going concern. As for you, since you're entered on the stock-list in a proper fashion, it's more than likely you'll be taken over with the stock."

What the big black-and-white cat said cheered the bears considerably. They didn't feel so sad when they learned the shop had been sold to a large firm in London.

"There's to be a manager called Mr. Wade," Boots told the others. "Mr. Shoehorn had used his letter as a bookmark in *The Shoemaker's Guide*, and I read it by mistake."

Boots didn't mention that the new manager's letter had seemed formal and abrupt and his signature pinched and neat.

Soon after, the cats brought news of a dinner to be given in honor of the retiring shopkeeper, and the bears felt so proud they forgot everything else.

"There's to be Windsor soup, turkey, and Christmas pudding," Hobson told them. "Our manager's putting in the turkey and pudding at a special price because it's so long after Christmas. They're having one of our best cheeses, port-type wine, muscatels and nuts, and fresh-ground coffee to follow."

"And Mr. Shoehorn's to be given a clock," added Little Tom. "It's in the back room of the jeweler's now. There are silver boots on each side of the dial, and a plate underneath which says it was given to Mr. Shoehorn on the occasion of his retirement by his fellow-tradesmen with affection and respect."

"The Bishop himself will be at the dinner," said Big Tom, "and all the oldest customers. They've taken the big room over the café that's usually used for weddings."

"We'll be able to see everything," said Little Tom, "because there's a skylight in the roof."

On the night of the dinner the cats made hourly reports to the bears, leaping to and fro across the rooftops.

"There are three long tables decorated with maidenhair ferns and pink carnations," reported Little Tom. "The Bishop said grace, and they're half-way through the soup."

"The Bishop has just given Mr. Shoehorn the clock," Hobson reported an hour later, "and Mr. Shoehorn's made his speech."

"He thanked them for everything," said Big Tom, "and he told them he has bought a bungalow by the sea where they will one and all be very welcome."

"Afterwards they clapped and clapped, and sang *For He's a Jolly Good Fellow*," said Hobson, "and someone took a picture of them all with Mr. Shoehorn in the center holding up the clock."

"It will be in *The Boot and Shoe Gazette*," said Big Tom, "and Mr. Shoehorn will have a special copy framed to hang over the clock."

One morning soon after the dinner, Mr. Shoehorn entered the shop accompanied by a tall man in a dark suit and black shoes. The newcomer's face was pale and solemn. Above his wrinkled forehead his hair was combed carefully over his domed head, as if each greased strand was counted and numbered. The bears guessed at once that it must be Mr. Wade, the new manager.

"You'll find these bears will look after your business very well," Mr. Shoehorn said with a smile, as he paused beside the bears to rub their furry heads. "I've found they keep the youngest children contented during the longest fitting."

"Indeed," said Mr. Wade, with barely a glance at the bears. "In my last establishment we found a tank of tropical fish much more effective and a good deal more hygienic." He frowned down at Socks, whose fur, in spite of constant brushing, bore clear traces of red ink and dark-tan shoe polish.

The bears felt very low when Mr. Shoehorn shut up the shop for the last time that night, and, with a final brush, left them together on their chair in the darkened shop.

"No one could have been kinder," Slippers said, as the last sound of the old shopkeeper's footsteps died away down the empty street.

"Or more considerate," added Boots, staring at the shopkeeper's shoehorn and measuring-stick, neatly arranged with his dusters and shoe brushes on a shelf below the counter. "There was never even a rough word in all those years, even at sale times."

Socks only sniffed, and the others pretended not to see as he rubbed his eye with one paw.

"We'll not see his like again," said Boots. "He was a true gentleman."

In all their thoughts was the memory of the new manager whom they had seen so briefly that afternoon.

"Of course we must be fair," said Boots. "Hasty judgment is always a mistake. He and Mr. Shoehorn had a lot to arrange. If he didn't seem over-cordial, he may have had a great deal on his mind."

"Or a stomach-ache," said Socks. "Only he needn't have said that about us not being hygienic, when we've been brushed and brushed, and Slippers has sprinkled us with so many mothballs we can hardly breathe."

Slippers sniffed. Not as Socks had sniffed, because he was sad, but to show her feelings.

"I know we've only seen him once," she said, "but if a shoe pinches the first time it's tried on it will go on pinching all the years it's worn—only worse."

Polly Trinket

MR. WADE arrived at the shoe shop the next day with the most bitter of northeast winds. The bears thought the new manager was like an east wind himself, changing and scattering everything in his path. He threw out all the old catalogs and disposed at cost-price of a great many shoes which he declared were old-fashioned. He described the bears in his new stock-list simply as *Sundry soft toys, juveniles, for the use of,* and he replaced the coal-fire in the hob-grate with electric radiators.

When the radiators were switched off at night, the bears shivered with cold. The linoleum felt like ice under their paws. Even in the daytime Mr. Wade left them in a gloomy corner at the back of the shop by the cash-desk. The bears' fur grew dusty, and Slippers fussed more and more about moths.

"We must be sensible," Boots told the others one night while they huddled close together to keep warm. "Even if Mr. Wade doesn't consider our feelings, he's an excellent shopkeeper. The sales have never been so good, especially between seasons. Dear Mr. Shoehorn was a shade set against some of the modern man-made fibers. Those new spring walking-shoes with the micro-cellular rubber soles should sell well, and they are astonishingly cheap."

Slippers only sneezed. Socks thumped her back, and dust flew into the chilly air.

"There you are," insisted Slippers. "He may be a good shopkeeper, but he hasn't brushed one of us for days and days. We'll be smothered in dust soon, and once it works down to the roots it's only a matter of time before the moths find out and move in."

Fortunately, it was their sad condition which brought about a change. One spring morning, as the sunlight shone into the shop, lighting up even their dark corner, Mr. Wade noticed the bears. He strode towards them with a frown and lifted Socks by one ear. As he held the small bear between his finger and thumb, motes of dust floated in the sunbeams, and two half-crushed mothballs tumbled to the floor.

"A disgraceful state of affairs," said the manager, sneezing hard. "I really must find extra help. The entire shop needs a proper spring cleaning."

That very morning a card appeared in the shop-window.

BOY WANTED FOR WORK IN SHOP. GOOD OPPORTUNITY FOR KEEN WORKER TO LEARN THE TRADE. NO PREVIOUS EXPERIENCE NECESSARY. SCHOOL-LEAVER WOULD SUIT.

The bears saw Polly Trinket for the first time that afternoon. She stood just inside the shop, with the sun shining on her straight carrot-red hair and her intent, freckled face. Her mouth was large and turned up at the corners. She wore a school blazer. It had shrunk from washing, and her reddened wrists protruded from the sleeves. Her shoes were cracked and worn, but they gleamed with polish. As Mr. Wade looked down at her from the other side of the counter, Polly seemed thinner and younger than ever, but she held her ground like a spindle-legged robin determined to retrieve a worm from under a gardener's fork.

"The card said you wanted a boy," said Polly

Trinket, "but I can work just as hard, and if you'll give me a trial you'll see."

The shopkeeper paused. Polly Trinket's thin hands were red and rough, as if they were well used to all kinds of housework. No one except a good polisher could have made the toe-caps of her shoes gleam so brightly.

"I hadn't thought of engaging a girl," said Mr. Wade doubtfully, "but since you've applied so promptly I'll consider it."

The bears listened breathlessly while Mr. Wade asked Polly questions.

"She's very small," Boots whispered, "hardly tall enough to reach the upper shelves for the sizes ten to twelve."

"She'll manage with the ladder," Socks said, "and for fitting shoes it's better to be small—there's not so far to bend."

"Hush!" said Slippers. "I'm sure Mr. Wade's going to engage her. Otherwise he wouldn't be showing her around the shop."

"It's help of a general nature I shall require," Mr. Wade told Polly. "Rush deliveries, keeping the shop dusted, and tidying the stock. Usually I shall attend to the customers, but when we are busy you must be ready to give a hand. Do you think you'll be able to manage all that?"

Polly turned to face him with shining eyes.

"Oh, yes, sir," she said. "It's always been shoes that have interested me. You see, my father was a shoemaker himself. Before he died, when I was twelve, he taught me how to handsew and heel. One of the shoes he re-welted and soled won a silver medal. We've the pair at home still, in a glass case. Ever since I was small I've meant to have a shoe shop of my own, with his name over the door. It will be just like this shop, only much bigger, with carpets soft as velvet and mirrors framed with gold."

Mr. Wade stared at the girl as she stood before him. The determination shining in her eyes disturbed him. It was as if at any moment she might step into his shoes and manage the business, leaving him with nothing to do

but retire. Possibly he had been mistaken and a boy would be a wiser choice. A lad might take less interest in the trade, but also be less trouble. Fortunately, at that moment Polly Trinket noticed the bears, and the spell was broken.

"What lovely bears!" she said. "I'll give them a good brush the very first thing." She lifted Slippers in her arms and smoothed the bear's silky fur. "I expect the children love to play with them while they're trying on their shoes."

"They're just a fancy of old Mr. Shoehorn, who used to own this shop," Mr. Wade told her, moving on impatiently. "In his day such methods may have seemed novel, but as soon as possible I intend to replace them with something more up to date, like a tank of tropical fish."

Polly didn't argue. She replaced Slippers and gave all the bears a quick hug before hurrying after Mr. Wade to inspect the stockroom.

Polly started work the next day. She brushed the bears' fur, blanket-stitched new flannel pads on Slippers's back paws, found a boot-button to replace one of the smallest bear's eyes which had been missing for weeks, and mended a split in the front seam of Boots's left leg so neatly that the stitches didn't even show. The bears had never looked so smart since they were new.

"She will go far," Boots declared. "She has just the same way with her younger customers as old Mr. Shoehorn."

Even the manager was pleased with his young assistant's industry. The whole shop shone with polish, and not a scrap of dust remained in the darkest corner. Once again the bears were seen in the front part of the shop. Polly put their basket-chair beside the showcase of children's shoes, and she fetched the bears for the younger customers. The bears sat proudly on the children's laps while their new spring shoes were chosen.

The daffodils bloomed and faded on the cathedral green, and summer came. Sandals and beach shoes hung outside the shop, and choirboys came for new cricket boots and tennis shoes. Polly Trinket wore a new cotton dress and a hat trimmed with buttercups and daisies.

The short nights were warm. Sometimes the cats from the cathedral called straight from their patrol under the summer stars, or Hobson dropped in from the grocer's next door, tired after the long day's work, with the scent of sawdust and bacon still clinging to his fur. The bears were always contented and full of praise for their new friend, Polly Trinket. Nowadays even Mr. Wade seemed less aloof.

"He fetched Slippers specially the other day for a little girl who was fidgeting," Boots told Hobson as the big cat lay relaxed on the cool linoleum, "and he hasn't said another word about replacing us with those tropical fish."

"And trade?" inquired Hobson, lazily licking one paw.

"It couldn't be better, said Boots proudly. "There's hardly a pair of light casuals or sandals to be marked down and sold off cheap at the end of the season."

One morning football boots stood in the shop-window ready for the new season. The lamb's-wool-lined boots were delivered with the fresh winter stock.

Unpacking a parcel of pink and blue angora bedsocks, Mr. Wade sneezed twice, and the day after he developed his first winter cold.

"Of course we can manage," Polly assured him when he arrived that morning looking pale, with a large package of paper handkerchiefs tucked under his arm. "Please go straight home till your cold's quite better."

Mr. Wade was too uncomfortable to notice that Polly Trinket had said *"we* can manage" instead of just "I." The bears had heard plainly enough, and they felt very proud.

"We must help her all we can," Boots told the others. After closing-time he and Slippers polished the floor with one of the best yellow dusters. Slippers sat on the duster and Boots pushed. Socks peered into shoe boxes and replaced their cardboard lids.

The rain fell in a steady stream, and there were few customers. The crate of children's rubber puddle-boots arrived at the shop on the second day of the manager's absence. The boots were of all colors. They shone as brightly as paint straight from a tube. Polly unpacked a pair of red boots, and, noticing Wellington Boots on his chair near by, she slipped the new boots onto his back paws. They fitted exactly. Polly took the big bear's front paws in her hands and stood him up. Boots balanced perfectly in the new red boots, and he stood very straight.

"Why, you look splendid!" said Polly, as her bright blue eyes met his own. "Everyone ought to see you in those boots. Then they would be sure to want some, too."

Polly set the bear back on the chair with the others,

and went to dust the display in the shop-window. Mr. Wade had left it set with men's walking-shoes, the football boots, and two display stands of shoe polish. With the rain streaming down the plate-glass outside, Polly thought the display looked as dull as any shop-window could look.

"I'll re-do it myself as a surprise for Mr. Wade when he comes back," Polly declared, smiling at the bears, "and you shall all be in it to advertise the boots."

She gave all the bears an extra brush. They were so excited, Socks whispered that he thought he felt sick, but Boots told him not to be silly. Polly found a strip of artificial grass in the stockroom which she spread in the shop-window. She set Wellington Boots on the grass to stride across it in his splendid boots.

"There are no boots small enough to fit either of you," Polly told the other bears when she had finally made the big bear balance properly, "but you can help just the same."

The bears watched while Polly arranged the other boots in the window and then sat down at the cash-desk with a paint-brush, a bottle of red ink, and all the largest pieces of white cardboard that she had been able to find. On the cards, in big red lettering, Polly wrote a set of slogans:

GO HOME HIGH AND DRY IN OUR NEW SEASON'S GUM BOOTS! BE LIKE THE BEARS AND WEAR BOOTS! COME IN NOW FOR A FITTING. AMPLE SUPPLIES, ALL SIZES NOW IN STOCK.

37

Polly put the cards in the window, and then she fetched the two smaller bears. She set Slippers in one corner, with her face mirrored in a puddle which was made from the looking-glass that usually hung in the cloakroom at the back of the shop. Polly put Socks in the very front of the window, with his upraised arm pointing to the largest sign of all, which bore the words: BEAR IT IN MIND. BUY BOOTS! in letters almost as large as the small bear himself.

All the passers-by paused outside the shop to stare at Polly's display. Over a dozen pairs of Wellington boots were sold the first day, and two dozen the next. The bears had never enjoyed themselves so much.

Hobson saw them from his own shop-window, where he often dozed beside a sack of coffee-beans and a display of the best Portuguese sardines, and once when no one was looking the bears waved at the cathedral cats, who had come to watch from the roof-tops across the Row.

Mr. Wade decided to come back to work on Saturday morning to make sure that all was well before the shop shut for the week-end. Boots caught sight of the manager first. As Mr. Wade hurried down the street he halted in his stride and stared at the shop-window as if unable to believe his eyes.

"Mr. Wade's coming now," whispered Boots, trying hard not to wobble in his excitement. "He still looks rather pale, but I expect that's just the surprise."

Mr. Wade stood in front of the window for a long time. He read all the slogans, and after he had finished he removed his spectacles, polished them, and studied

the advertisements again. With the manager's eye upon them, Socks tried hard not to giggle, and Slippers never raised her eyes from the puddle. Polly stood smiling in the shop behind them, and they were determined to do her credit.

When Mr. Wade finally banged open the door and strode frowning into the shop, even Boots nearly toppled over, and Socks's upraised paw slipped slowly down to his side. They had never heard anyone sound so angry before.

"Please remove those slogans and the bears from my shop-window instantly," Mr. Wade told Polly Trinket. "In this part of the town, where trading has always been carried on in a dignified and seemly fashion, I am appalled to see what you have done, and I have seldom seen anything more gaudy or distasteful."

The smile on Polly's face faded as if a light had gone out, but her red hair was still bright like a flag in the gloomy winter light.

"But I thought it would brighten the window up," Polly protested. "Everyone else has liked it and stopped to look. Even the Bishop looked at the bears for ages. He bought a pair of blue boots for his grand-niece specially, and we've sold nearly all the others. We haven't been so busy since the summer sale."

Mr. Wade sat down and wiped his pale forehead with a hemstitched handkerchief.

"No doubt you meant very well," he said, "but in a business such as this, new-fangled stunts are quite out of place. Our sales have always been made through the quality of our merchandise, aided possibly by a discreetly worded advertisement in the parish magazine, but no more, and certainly not those bears."

When Polly lifted Boots from the shop-window and pulled off his red Wellingtons, the big bear felt a single tear drop on the top of his head. All that bleak and gloomy day Polly went about her work in silence with a handkerchief crumpled in her hand. Now and then she sniffed.

The bears sat once more in the dark corner at the back of the shop. Few customers came in except an old lady for some bedroom slippers, and a man for a tin of dark-tan shoe polish. Mr. Wade redressed the window with men's walking-shoes and a single pair of gleaming riding-boots.

"There's a fox's mask in the stockroom and some cork-chips that look like earth," Polly suggested, when he had nearly finished, but Mr. Wade only added the last price-tags and told her the display would do very well as it was.

After the manager had gone home, with barely a word to Polly, she paused beside the bears as she buttoned her coat and tied a scarf over her head.

"Poor old bears," she said. "You've had a beastly day, too. If I were you I wouldn't work any more for someone who was so horrid and ungrateful. I only stay myself because I need the money and I want to be a shoe-shop keeper myself one day, so I have to stay and learn."

After Polly had gone the bears sat thinking of her words. Wellington Boots felt suddenly old, and the hair around his muzzle was thin. Slippers rested her head against the larger bear's shoulder. She knew how much Boots had enjoyed wearing the red Wellington boots. To take a leading part in the running of the shoe shop he loved so much had meant more to the big bear than it had meant to any of them. The manager's words had hurt his feelings badly.

"Polly's right," Boots said at last. "If our services are no longer needed or valued here it's stupid for us to stay."

Slippers hated change, but she put her paw gently on his and spoke bravely.

"No doubt you're right, Boots dear. We'll find other work. Perhaps Hobson would know of a situation, or the cathedral cats."

"We might help with a Christmas toy-bazaar," suggested Socks, "or sit advertising the dry-cleaner's."

Boots sat silent with a faraway look in his eyes.

"What I should like best," he said, "is not to find other employment but to retire like old Mr. Shoehorn. We've all of us worked for the best years of our lives, and none of us is as young as he once was. Now it would be nice to take things easy and find a place where we could sit and think."

"But how could we do that?" Slippers asked. The shop was very cold, and she felt tired. When Mr. Wade finally replaced them with tropical fish, she didn't know what would become of them all. What might happen was more frightening even than moths, and she shivered.

"I don't know how," Boots said. "Probably once you're a working bear that's how you have to stay till you're too old to do it any more."

Beside them Socks sat up. His ginger fur gleamed in the dim light.

"It isn't," he said. "I know what we can do. We must find ourselves proper homes. For ages children have just played with us while they're in the shop; now we must find a family who will look after us for always."

Socks and a Shopping-Basket

"OF COURSE we shall have to think about what we mean to do very carefully," Boots remarked to the others when they woke the next morning. "None of us knows exactly what a real home is like. After all the excitement of an active business life, we might find it rather dull and cramping."

"And there's no point in leaping out of the frying-pan into the fire," Slippers agreed drowsily. "For many reasons I should be happy enough to remain here in a place we've always known."

"And loved," said Boots, gazing fondly around the shop.

On Sunday morning the bears had the shop to themselves. The cathedral bells rang cheerfully, and the rain had stopped. The bears snoozed in the autumn sunlight and entertained their friends. Telling Hobson and Big Tom and Little Tom the whole story of their sudden banishment from the shop-window made them feel much less upset. The cats enjoyed every word, only

43

interrupting now and then to say, "Did you ever!" "Just like him!" "I should think so!" and "What nerve!"

In the end the cats were so loud in their disapproval of the shopkeeper that Boots, especially, found himself speaking up in his defense.

"Of course, as manager, he was within his rights. Possibly Polly in her youth and enthusiasm went a little too far. Mr. Shoehorn himself was doubtful, very doubtful indeed, about the more flashy forms of advertising. There was talk once of a neon sign and his name in lights, but he very soon came out against it, and I am sure that he was right."

By Monday morning only Socks was as determined as ever to make a change, whatever the consequences. He didn't care what the others said about being cautious. In fact, it was Slippers's remark about leaping out of the frying-pan which in the end gave Socks his idea.

It was a fine, frosty morning, and the shop was full of customers. Mr. Wade's cold had disappeared. After selling several pairs of the most expensive snow-boots, he was in the best of tempers. He smiled most kindly at Polly when he called her forward to serve a customer who had just entered the shop with two flaxen-haired little girls, and a baby of about eighteen months in her arms.

"Mrs. Brown wants plimsolls* for her little girls," he told Polly, "and a pair of red leather shoes for the baby."

Polly was delighted to serve Mrs. Brown and her family. She settled Mrs. Brown comfortably in a chair with the baby on her knee, and put the housewife's

* canvas shoes

44

heavy shopping-basket on the floor beside her. Before measuring the children's feet with her size-stick, Polly fetched the bears. The two little girls played with Boots and Slippers throughout the fitting. The baby had Socks, but the little boy was much more interested in the shoes Polly brought for him to try on, and the small bear lay forgotten in the folds of his pram rug.

"Now we must hurry home to lunch," said Mrs. Brown when all the shoes were finally chosen and the baby sat kicking happily in his old shoes while the new ones were wrapped. "Thank this young lady for taking so much trouble, Sally and Sarah, and say good-bye to the bears."

With a final hug the girls handed Boots and Slippers back to Polly Trinket. She bundled the bears under her arm as she waited to hand her customer the parcels of shoes, the receipted bill, and the change.

Sarah and Sally ran to open the shop door. As their mother wrapped the excited toddler in his pram rug, Boots and Slippers under Polly's arm stiffened. Hidden in a fold of the rug they had caught sight of the small, forgotten ginger bear. For a moment, as Mrs. Brown stood up with the baby in her arms, Socks hung precariously by one paw. Then he dived head first into the darkness of the shopping-basket, which stood beside her chair.

"Bring my basket, there's good girls," Mrs. Brown told her daughters, as she hurried out to the pram with the baby. With the heavy basket held between them, the girls ran to join their mother. Boots and Slippers watched speechless from Polly's arms while the basket

was loaded onto the pram, the children waved good-bye, and the pram, with Socks aboard, was wheeled rapidly away down Cordwainer's Row.

Even when Boots and Slippers were alone during the lunch hour, they felt almost too surprised and dazed to talk about what had occurred. Mr. Wade always lunched in the café in the High Street, and Polly ate sandwiches on the cathedral green, scattering crumbs over the pages of *The Footwear Retailer's Manual*.

"It's an opportunity for Socks, of course," Slippers

observed at last, as she and Boots sat together in the empty shop. "We should feel happy for him. He couldn't have chosen a better family—only when we talked about finding a proper home I never thought of one of us going alone and leaving the others."

Boots sniffed crossly. He was worried about Socks and annoyed with him, too, for making Slippers miserable.

"Naturally he will be brought back," he told Slippers. "He should have guessed that himself. What he's done was just impulsive and ridiculous. He should at least have consulted us first before taking such a step, not just gone off without so much as a wave or good-bye."

"But he hadn't time," argued Slippers, "and it wasn't a step he took but more of a nose-dive. He had to decide just in a second, and then do it so that no one saw. Even Polly never noticed he had gone at all."

"She will directly she tidies up," said Boots. "Then there will be a fine fuss. Very likely they'll tell the police."

Boots hunched his shoulders and sat scowling straight at the black blob which was the tip of his nose.

"The smallest of those teddy bears is missing," Polly reported to the manager soon after the shop reopened after lunch. "He was here this morning because I gave him to Mrs. Brown's baby to hold, but now I can't find him anywhere."

"No doubt the little chap tossed him somewhere into a corner," Mr. Wade told her, without looking up from the crossword puzzle he had been unable to finish during lunch. "I expect he'll turn up in good time. Even if he's gone for good it's not a very great loss."

In spite of the manager's indifference, Polly searched everywhere for the bear, and like Slippers and Boots she kept an expectant watch on the shop door, in case someone should hurry in to return the missing bear. By closing-time no one had arrived, and the mystery of the small bear's disappearance was unsolved.

"I'll have a real search tomorrow," Polly whispered to the bears before she went home that night. "Don't you worry. He must be somewhere."

When Hobson and the cathedral cats looked in later that evening as usual, Boots and Slippers felt a little better. They seldom had anything startling to tell the cats, and though their news was sad it was still news.

"You'll never guess what's happened," said Slippers, the moment she and Boots saw the cats poised on the edge of the skylight. "Socks has gone!"

"To a real family who were in the shop this morning," added Boots. "When they got up to leave Socks just dived into their shopping-basket and was taken away."

"Well, I never!" said Hobson. "Good for him!"

They talked to the cats for a long time in the moonlit shop. They told them of their decision to make a change and to seek homes of their own.

"But we never thought Socks would arrange something so soon," said Boots.

"Or do it alone," added Slippers. "Naturally we want the very best for the little fellow, only we miss him dreadfully already, and if the family keeps him it will

48

be awful to think we may never set eyes on him again."

There wasn't much that Hobson or Big Tom and Little Tom could say. They sat with their paws folded and their heads bent and their ears twitching as they listened to every word.

"You mustn't worry," Hobson told Slippers, when they finally rose to leave. "Socks is a sensible little chap with his wits about him. He'll manage, even out there."

The bears stared up through the skylight at the great domed sky. The world which lay beyond the shelter of the shoe shop they had always known seemed very large, especially for one adventurous ginger bear.

After the cats had gone Boots and Slippers sat in the darkness for a long time. Both of them were thinking about Socks and what might have happened to him.

"If he ever comes back," Slippers began, suddenly breaking the long silence, "if we ever see Socks again . . ."

"Of course he'll come back and we'll see him again," said Boots firmly. "Even if the Browns didn't bring him back today, they're sure to do it tomorrow. A family like that wouldn't just keep a bear without even asking."

"Well, when Socks comes back," continued Slippers, "if we still want to move and find a home of our own, let's only do it together. Being split up is worse than anything after we've all been together for so long."

In the darkness Boots put his paw on hers.

"Of course we'll stay together," he said, and, comforted by his promise, Slippers fell asleep.

The policeman on his rounds halted outside the shoe shop late that night. He shone his flashlight as usual over the interior of the shop, and saw the two bears together on their basket-chair. Tonight something was different, and he swung the light back on to the sleeping bears.

"Upon my soul," he said to himself, "the smallest bear is missing. In all the years I've passed here there have always been three. Where on earth can the little ginger bear have got to?"

The police constable tested the padlocked door, and, finding it secure, he went on his way with a puzzled frown.

What Happened to Socks

Socks LANDED upside down in the shopping-basket on top of a carton of new-laid eggs. Mrs. Brown's basket was deep and made of woven rushes. Inside it Socks was invisible, except for the tip of his back paw poking up between a bag of doughnuts and some pink knitting-wool. Even the baby hadn't noticed Socks dive into the basket. Through a small hole in the side of the basket Socks could just see him as he sat clutching his new shoes and smiling as his mother pushed the pram swiftly on its way.

Sarah and Sally trotted on either side of the pram. Socks hoped the two sisters would like him. In the shop they had clearly enjoyed playing with the bigger bears, but from the first Socks had done his best to keep out of sight, hidden in the folds of the baby's rug. The toddler himself had helped by wriggling so much that for a while he had been sitting almost on top of the small bear.

"Of course they'll like me," Socks decided, as the

pram jolted down a curb and the basket tilted so that he found himself sitting on a bag of bull's-eyes and a pound of pork sausages. "I may not be as large as Boots, or as handsome as Slippers, but at least I'll be a surprise."

When the Browns came to a small house on the outskirts of the town, a puppy bounced down the garden path to greet them.

Inside the shopping-basket Socks stiffened. The puppy was black and white. Shaggy fur tumbled over his brown eyes, and his white teeth looked needle-sharp.

"Dogs don't hurt you unless you are silly and tease them," Socks said stoutly to himself. "And this one is no more than a puppy." But as Mrs. Brown set down the basket on the porch while she carried the baby indoors, Socks felt far smaller than usual.

While the children helped their mother unload the pram, the puppy jumped up to investigate the contents of the basket. A moment later the basket toppled over, and Socks was a prisoner between the excited puppy's paws. He lay quite still, with the dog's pink tongue only an inch from his eyes.

"Oh, Bouncer, what have you done now?" cried Mrs. Brown, as she ran to pick up the groceries. "You really are the naughtiest puppy! And what have you got there?"

"It's a toy bear," said Sarah, rescuing Socks from the puppy not a second too soon. "Do come and look, Sally. He must have been in the basket, but how he got there I can't think."

Socks held his breath as they all stared at him. He knew if they guessed he came from the shop his adventure would end and he would be taken back almost at once. Luckily his efforts to keep out of sight in the shoe shop had proved successful. Only the baby chuckled on catching sight of him again, and he was too young to tell.

"It is a puzzle," said Mrs. Brown, as Sally and her sister wiped Socks clean and smoothed his ginger fur. "He's such a dear little bear that someone is sure to be really fond of him and missing him right now. We'll have to try and find out who it is. When Daddy comes home tomorrow we'll ask him if anyone has inquired for a lost bear at the station, and in the meantime we must take good care of him."

Socks was puzzled why anyone should ask for a lost bear at the railway-station, but he was too pleased and excited with his new surroundings to pay the remark much attention.

Sally and Sarah couldn't have been kinder to Socks. As he said long afterwards, they treated him like a visiting royal monarch. In their playroom were wonderful objects of whose existence he had not even dreamt. There was a whole house made specially small for dolls, though it fitted a bear of Socks's size just as well. There was a pram just like the baby's, only smaller, and a wooden engine with a whistle, which Socks could drive. Perched in the driver's place, with one arm waving and the other on the controls, Socks had never felt so happy before.

At lunch he sat between the girls. His place was laid with a doll's plate edged with pink roses. The baby grinned and waved a spoonful of sieved spinach. Some of it spattered the bear's fur, and Sarah wiped him clean with a handkerchief printed with a picture of Goldilocks and the three bears.

Yet, in spite of their kindness, as the day wore on Socks felt something he had never felt before. The feeling crept over him like a cloud shadowing grassland. He missed the other bears. He missed Boots, who, whatever happened, always knew exactly what to do. From his long life in the shop, Boots knew how to deal, in a polite and dignified fashion, with puppies who jumped up and sniffed. He was never upset or shy. Without

Boots, Socks felt as if a brick wall against which he had been leaning had suddenly fallen down. Socks missed Slippers even more. By the evening he missed her so much it felt like an ache which filled his whole stuffed body.

At bedtime Socks wished with all his heart that he hadn't been quite so careful to keep out of sight that morning in the shop. Surely one of the children might have noticed him. As Sally and her sister prepared for bed, Socks longed for one of them to look at him and say, "Of course, I remember now where the little bear belongs. He was in the shoe shop where we bought our shoes."

But even when the children took off their new plimsolls and sniffed their brand-new rubber soles, neither of them spoke.

Socks pictured the shoe shop in Cordwainer's Row closing for the first time without him. He remembered the smell of boot polish, leather bootlaces, and leather, and the comfortable "camphor" smell of the bears themselves. Ever since he had first come to the shoe shop, Socks had always slept between Boots and Slippers on the basket-chair, and now neither of them was with him.

"Having a new bear to play with has been fun," Sally remarked, as she looked at Socks sitting alone on the bedside table, "only I wish we knew where he really belongs. I'm sure he's lonely and wants to go back."

"Daddy's certain to be able to help," said Sarah. "I shouldn't worry. Daddy notices everything that happens in Slumber Lightly, even if it's only about bears."

Socks slept at last, comforted by her words. When

55

he woke it was morning. Sarah and Sally were sitting up in bed.

"There's Daddy coming in now," said Sally. "We'll ask him about the bear at once."

A moment later a man stood smiling in the doorway, in answer to their call. Socks realized in a flash the explanation to Mrs. Brown's remark which had puzzled him the day before. It wasn't at the railway-station she had meant that inquiries would be made for a missing bear, but at the police-station. The children's father, who had just come off duty, was a policeman, and the very one who patrolled each night past the shoe shop in Cordwainer's Row.

After the children had told him about their discovery of the bear, Mr. Brown took Socks in his large hand and studied him carefully for a long time. Socks might have been as valuable and important as a long-lost diamond necklace.

"Of course I know where he belongs," he said with a smile. "I happened to notice one of them was missing only tonight. He's the smallest of the three bears who live in the shoe shop in Cordwainer's Row, and you'd better take him back first thing this morning."

When the children and Mrs. Brown hurried into the shoe shop soon after breakfast, Mr. Wade was too busy ordering the next season's sandals to pay much attention to their explanation and apology. Only Polly looked pleased, and thanked them for returning the small bear.

"So you're back," said Boots, without even turning his head, when Polly put Socks once more with the others on the basket-chair. "Slippers and I were wondering if you would turn up. The cats were around last night. Big Tom wasn't too hopeful when he heard what you'd done. He thought most likely you would end up on the threepenny stall at a jumble sale."

"We've worried dreadfully," said Slippers. "If you'd stayed away even another day we couldn't have borne it." She looked fondly at the small bear seated between them.

Socks's face looked a trifle worn, and one ear hung loose where it had come unstitched.

"I've been to a real home," he said, ignoring Boots's frosty reception. "I went in the shopping-basket. It was easy as winking."

"I hope the home proved as pleasant as you expected?" Boots asked stiffly.

"It did," said Socks. "I had a splendid time, only I missed you and Slippers. I missed you both so much it ached inside. I wouldn't want to be in a home ever again unless we could be together to enjoy it."

The scowl on Boots's face faded, and Slippers sniffed.

"Well, since you're back, and you're the only one who has been to a real home, I suppose you might as well tell us about it," said Boots. He still sat up very straight and dignified, but he bent his head so that his eyes looked down kindly at the small bear.

"Yes, please do," begged Slippers. "Then we'll know if we would really like to find one for ourselves or not."

In the shop, looking at the shelves lined with boxes labeled *Gents' Brown Oxo, Maids' Mid-Tan Casuals, Ladies' Glacé Courts,* and *Youths' Suède Monks,* Socks suddenly didn't know where to begin. The cash-desk, with the bottle of red ink for sale labels and the collection-box for the cathedral fabric fund, the showcase with feathered mules and silver slippers, the tins of shoe polish and cards of laces, were all part of another world. Socks remembered the scent of sausages and rice pudding, the baby's blue high-chair, with chipped yellow ducklings parading along the back, the dolls' house, and the battered wooden engine. Socks knew that a home like the one he had seen was the best place for a bear to be. But an icy wind shook the OPEN sign on the shop door, and already his brief visit seemed like a fast-fading dream.

"Tell us everything from the very beginning," Slippers prompted. "Mr. Wade is still fussing over the orders, and Polly is tidying the stockroom. They won't interrupt."

So Socks began.

"It was being warm I noticed most. There was a coal-fire in the living room and a gasfire in the bedroom, but it wasn't just the fires that made you warm; it was being with them all. Inside their house was like being in a box with kittens tumbling around the mother cat and every one purring because there has been plenty of milk." Socks hesitated. The listening bears looked puzzled, but he tried to go on. "At teatime, they didn't have just a cup brought around from the café with a saucer on top; they sat down at a table. There was bread and butter, and doughnuts, and honey just for me. The girls spread it on a rusk, and they gave me a doll's cup with roses all around, full of real tea."

"That was silly; they should have known bears don't

need to eat or drink," interrupted Slippers. She thought there was no need for Socks to talk about the little girls as if no one had bothered to look after him properly in his life before.

"Of course they knew," retorted Socks. "It was a game. The puppy had everything afterwards."

"You didn't say there was a dog before," observed Boots. "Was that how your ear came unsewn?"

Socks ignored the question. He didn't care to be reminded of the puppy.

"After tea we watched the television," he continued quickly. "They rent the set and it has a seventeen-inch screen."

"What was on?" Boots asked casually, with his eyes on one upturned foot. "Just that silly old tuning-chart

with the lines and circles?" Some time ago a radio shop had opened across the way, and the bears had viewed snatches of the programs on a demonstration set in the shop-window.

"Cowboys," replied Socks. "Everyone banged guns and galloped. The Red Indians galloped fastest of all, and they yelled blood-curdling cries."

"Weren't you scared?" Slippers asked with a shiver.

"Of course not," said Socks. "It wasn't half so loud as the guns on the shooting-gallery where I was won."

Everything Socks described convinced the others that a home was where they ought to be. Slippers marveled over a mothproof hanging wardrobe in which the children's summer clothes were kept, and Boots wanted more and more details about the cowboys and the wooden engine. They talked right through the lunch hour while Polly Trinket sat with her head bent over a textbook, memorizing the names of the different kinds of nails used in hobnailing the sole of a boot: bullet, Victoria, Star, Cress, Welsh Square, marble, clasp, Irish, square, fancy square, and fancy crab. Few of their customers wore hob-nailed boots, but Polly was determined to be prepared.

The bears talked long after the shop was shut. They talked far into the night, but still none of them could think of a way to find a home of their own.

"We shall in the end, you'll see," said Boots, with a yawn, when they finally settled down. "Where there's a will there's always a way, and if we think and think we're bound to find it."

Stowaways

ONE DAY in mid-December, when the shop lights had to be lit by three o'clock and the first snowflakes fluttered in the northeast wind outside the window, a truck edged its way slowly down Cordwainer's Row. In the truck lay a great, rustling spruce tree, so wide that the needles on the tips of the branches brushed the shop-windows.

"It's a huge Christmas tree," said Slippers, as the bears peered after the truck. "The biggest I've ever seen. The truck has stopped by the green, and they're unloading the tree outside the cathedral."

It was a Wednesday, when the shop shut early at one o'clock. Usually the bears disliked early-closing days when the shop was closed for so long, but today the great spice-scented tree with its springing branches excited and pleased them, and they were glad to be alone. They longed to bounce in the foliage and nose their way through the resin-scented needles.

All that afternoon they watched while the tree was

set up on the grass before the great west doors of the cathedral. When the tree was finally in place it stood dark and tall, with the lighted cathedral window shining through the branches and the stars high overhead.

"Will the tree grow there always?" Socks asked. He was perched on Boots's shoulders to see more clearly through the glass-topped shop door.

The big bear stood himself on two shoe boxes which bent under his weight.

"Of course not, silly," said Boots. "It's specially for Christmas."

The cats dropped in that night, full of information about the tree. Big Tom's and Little Tom's sleek black fur smelled of the spruce-needles, and their claws were sharp where they had sharpened them on the rough bark. Even Hobson, who was heavy from good feeding on bacon bones and ham, had inspected each twig and branch minutely.

"It was the Bishop's idea," Big Tom told the bears. "The tree came all the way from Canada, and it's to be hung with gifts."

"For deserving families in the diocese," added Little Tom. "Everyone is being asked to give something—toys and sweets and things to eat. All the presents will be hung on the tree, and, after a carol service the day before, they'll be taken down and delivered on Christmas Eve."

"Mrs. Saltmarsh is chairman of the committee, and she is going around with a list asking," said Hobson. "She came to us yesterday. The manager is giving two tins of Best Mixed Chocolate Biscuits, two jars of Pekin ginger, half a dozen boxes of crackers with caps and novelties, and a Yuletide log cake."

"I expect she'll call here soon," added Big Tom. "She went to the church shop last week. The manager hadn't anything to offer except two brass vases and a board for hymn numbers, but the girl who does the typing offered to make stuffed animals from the bits left over from the hassocks."

"She's made a grey elephant you'd hardly tell from real," said Hobson, "with a saddle all scarlet and gold."

"The Bishop's grand-niece has given a package of pink-sugar mice we thought most pleasing," said Big Tom, "and the Verger's wife is knitting socks."

The bears listened to all the cats told them, and they thought of all the homes which would be happier that Christmas because of the Bishop's tree.

Mrs. Saltmarsh arrived with her list the very next day. She was tall and grey-haired, dressed in a tweed deer-stalker hat, a lamb's-wool-lined jacket, corduroy slacks, and a pair of Mr. Shoehorn's finest hand-sewn brogue shoes. Mrs. Saltmarsh carried a shooting-stick with a sharp point. She eyed Mr. Wade across the counter as if she were riding and facing a water-splash beyond a thorn fence.

"Ah, Mr. Wade," she said, "I've come to ask you what you will be kind enough to give us for the Bishop's Christmas tree. All the traders in the town have been most generous in their support, and I know you will be as well."

Mr. Wade smiled a small, tight smile, which never reached as far as his eyes. Mrs. Saltmarsh's keen blue eyes were already inspecting his stock. He saw her gaze halt beside the showcase of children's fur-lined slippers and silver dancing-pumps.

"It would be something for the kiddies that you would want, I expect," said Mr. Wade doubtfully. "I hardly think in a shop such as this we have much that would be suitable. Toys and playthings are really not in our line."

"Not at all, Mr. Wade," Mrs. Saltmarsh corrected him, with the same firm patience she would have shown to a horse hesitating before a difficult jump. "For older children, anything new and pretty to wear would be most welcome, and of course we shall not forget the older folk. Warm feet make a warm heart, as old Mr. Shoehorn always used to say."

As she spoke her eyes were fixed on a pair of lamb's-wool-lined boots, which stood on display beside a label declaring that they would make a Very Acceptable Xmas Gift. Mr. Wade cleared his throat, adjusted his tie, and frowned at Polly, who had printed the labels and scattered them liberally around the shop. The boots cost five pounds.

"Naturally, at this festive season I should be glad to help in any way I can," said Mr. Wade. "You will understand that if any considerable outlay is involved I would have to consult my company, but I have some kiddies' bedroom slippers put aside in the stockroom, which I am sure I might let you have. They're nice, serviceable little slippers, but a line that's selling a trifle slowly, so I think I can safely promise half a dozen pairs."

After Mrs. Saltmarsh had gone, the manager told Polly to pack the bedroom slippers in a large box. The slippers Mr. Wade had donated were made of drab checked cloth, with ankle straps and bone buttons. Though the cloth looked thick and clumsy, it was only made from waste wool yarn and cotton, which had little warmth. Mr. Wade had set the slippers aside some time ago, to be sold off in the sale.

"It's a shame," Polly remarked to the bears, as she knelt beside the box. "Children who are poor and won't have many presents ought to be given the very prettiest slippers we have. Mr. Wade's just as mean as he can be." Her cheerful face was clouded, as if she knew only too well how such children might feel.

Polly left the box ready in the stockroom, but she didn't fasten down the lid. Before it was sent to the cathedral, she hoped Mr. Wade might change his mind and tell her to replace the slippers with some of their best slippers made of velvet and decorated with gold.

Polly Trinket seemed worried about other things besides the slippers. Her face was pale and thin, and each night she hurried home with hardly a word to the bears. Once she was late, and the bears thought her eyes looked red, as if she had been crying. Instead of reading textbooks during her lunch hour, she spent the time scurrying from shop to shop buying groceries or mending children's clothes. In every spare moment she was sewing on buttons, darning the frayed elbows of jumpers, patching faded jeans, and mending socks.

"She's fussed and upset," remarked Slippers, after Polly had been in trouble for forgetting a message and sending a customer home with the wrong pair of shoes. "It's not just Mr. Wade's sharpness. Her mind's not on her work. She jumps every time the telephone rings or the shop door opens, and the moment the shop shuts she runs all the way home. Hobson thinks they must be in trouble. She buys all the cheapest foods and never wastes a penny on cakes or jam."

"And the cathedral cats say she never goes out to the dance hall or the movies," said Socks. "Once she's home, the lights are on till all hours. They've seen her baking and shaking mops and ironing till past ten o'clock."

For once Wellington Boots didn't seem interested in someone else's troubles.

"Possibly she's just tired of this job and wants a change," he suggested. "I shouldn't worry. A girl as bright and intelligent as Polly should have no difficulty in bettering herself, especially at her age."

Boots's voice was wistful. The others knew he also longed to make a change. Boots didn't say a great deal about their decision to find a home, even to the cats, but the others knew he was still puzzling over the problem and that he would never give up until what they hoped to do was safely accomplished.

Every day the big bear sat for hours with his eyes fixed on the Christmas tree at the end of the street. As Christmas drew nearer, down Cordwainer's Row came more and more people with gifts for the tree. Mrs. Brown and her children hurried past the shop with their pram piled high with toys they had made and a big bunch of balloons they had blown up themselves.

"Tomorrow they'll hang all the presents on the tree," Big Tom told the bears when he arrived one night. "The Bishop's palace is crammed with them. You can see them piled on all the chairs through the windows."

"There's everything that anyone could want," said Little Tom.

In the corner Boots sat listening. When he spoke his voice was casual, as if he didn't really mind about the answer or not.

"Did you happen to notice," he asked, "if there were any bears?"

Big Tom glanced at the smaller cat.

"Not that we noticed," said Little Tom. "Dolls, we saw dozens of, and cowboy suits, and trains, but I don't recollect any bears."

In the corner Boots's eyes shone bright, but he said no more.

When the cats had gone Socks and Slippers missed the larger bear. They discovered him in the stockroom carefully inspecting the box into which Polly had packed the slippers which were to be given for the tree. As they watched, Boots lay down on the floor beside the box, and, seeing the others, he told them to do it too.

"But why?" argued Slippers. "The floor's dusty, and we've just been brushed."

"Never mind why," said Boots. "Just do it. I'll lie on the bottom, and you and Socks balance on top."

The others did as he asked without further argument.

"Just as I thought," Boots said triumphantly, as Socks lost his balance and they all sat up. "We should all fit in with a bit to spare."

"Fit in where?" asked Socks.

"Into the box, of course," said Boots. "Tomorrow Polly's taking it to be put on the tree, and instead of those bedroom slippers inside, there will be us!"

The others stared. They had always respected Boots and his sound common sense, but they had never admired him so much as they did at that moment.

"You mean we will be put with all the other presents on the Christmas tree and given to children who really need us?" asked Socks.

"Of course," said Boots. "Once we're on the tree there won't be anything to do but sit and sit till we're taken away. It's the best chance we'll ever have to find a good home of our own."

"But will we be sent somewhere together?" Slippers asked doubtfully. "You know how Socks felt before, and we've always said we wouldn't be parted again."

She laid her flattened plush paw on the bigger bear's arm, and he patted it.

"I thought of that," said Boots. "We'll fasten ourselves together with that string they use to keep the beach shoes in pairs. Everyone will know then that we're meant to keep together as a family-set."

While the bears knotted the string around one another they thought of the tree in whose branches they would hang the next day. They imagined their first Christmas in a real home of their own. Always before, their shop had been shut at Christmas for three long days, and they had been alone. Even the cats would not be there to visit them, for Hobson was always taken home by the man in charge of the bacon counter, and the cathedral cats stayed by the gasfire in the Verger's lodge, feasting off turkey giblets and cream left over from the choristers' Christmas dinner. The bears had always tried to make the best of it. Slippers collected the sprigs of artificial holly used for decorating the shop-window, Socks made paper caps from the bags in which small purchases were wrapped, and Boots told jokes which he found on the backs of matchboxes, but they had always been glad when the holiday was over and the shop re-opened for the January sale.

There was too much to do to think about their future good fortune for long. The bedroom slippers the box still contained had to be tipped out and concealed in the stockroom behind some beach sandals which wouldn't be disturbed until the spring. At last the bears were all safely hidden inside the box.

"Now all we need to do is wait," said Boots with a sigh, as Slippers pulled several sheets of tissue paper neatly over their heads and Socks let down the lid.

At first, shut inside the large cardboard box, the bears tried to sleep, but they were all too excited. In the end they talked till the first rays of light shone into the stock-room, and they knew the day of their adventure had dawned.

At ten minutes past nine Polly ran into the shop. Her coat was unbuttoned, and snowflakes lay unmelted in her tangled hair.

"Really, Miss Trinket," declared the manager with a frown, "when there is so much to do I think you

should be on time. No, don't take off your coat. There
are a number of errands I shall want you to do. Several
of our country customers have been unable to come in
because of the snow, and I have promised to send off
their requirements from the bus depot; there are some
accounts to be delivered by hand; and these Christmas
cards to be stamped and posted."

"And shall I take the box of slippers for the Bishop's
tree?" Polly asked. "They want all the parcels there
well before the carol service at three o'clock."

"By all means take it down with you as you will be passing," agreed Mr. Wade. "Only do make haste."

Polly ran into the stockroom and knelt beside the box. Inside the bears clasped each other with their stiff paws. None of them dared to breathe as Polly smoothed the paper covering them and secured the lid. With the box balanced on the top of her other packages, and the snow falling thick and fast around her, Polly raced down Cordwainer's Row, carrying the three bears on the first part of their journey to happiness and freedom.

My Lord Bishop

No ONE unpacked the bears. Their box was hung with the other parcels on the tree, so that the falling snow would not damage the contents. The bears had hoped to sit in the gaily decorated branches, waving proudly to their friends and admired by all the spectators. However, even inside the box they could feel the branches springing under them, and through a crack in one corner they were able to see most of what was happening. They took turns to look, and reported what they saw to the others.

"Dozens and dozens more parcels have come," Socks told his friends. "Boy Scouts are piling them around the foot of the tree, and there are heaps more on the cathedral porch."

Once he caught sight of Big Tom and Little Tom, who had halted to inspect the tree on their way across the snowy grass.

"Look at us," Socks shouted, jumping about so that the box swayed on its cord. "Boots and Slippers and I are all inside the box from the shoe shop. We're going to a proper home where children really need us."

The small bear's voice was muffled by the wrappings, and the two cats never heard. They flicked the snow from their paws and slipped through the narrow, padded side door into the cathedral, where they sat under the tattered flags over a grill that puffed warm air into the building, and watched for mice.

"I wish we could have told them and Hobson," Slippers remarked. "It's a shame to leave without saying good-bye."

"Directly we're settled we'll get word to them and have a house-warming," Boots told her comfortably.

After lunch more and more people gathered around the tree, waiting for the carol service to begin. The children were muffled in scarves. They stamped their fur-lined boots in the trodden snow and huddled close to the tree, as if even in the ice-cold wind the glittering decorations gave them warmth.

Just when Socks was beginning to fidget, and Slippers was thinking that their box swayed rather too much in the wind, and Boots was ready to snap at them both, the main doors of the cathedral swung open, and the clergy and choristers trooped out.

"There's the Bishop," Slippers whispered, "right in the center, with the shepherd's crook in his hand. You can just see he's wearing some of our rubber boots under his surplice."

The snow fell on the choristers' bared heads, on the Bishop's shoulders and the jeweled arms of the processional cross. It settled on the round spectacles of the youngest choirboy, on the flowered hat of the Lady Mayoress, on Mrs. Saltmarsh's wind-tanned face, on the helmets of the police and the bowed heads of the oldest pensioners in the town. It settled on old and young and rich and poor, but no one cared, for in their center was the tree, with its branches weighed down by their gifts.

In the cold, clear silence of the mid-winter afternoon a choirboy sang the first verse of the opening carol.

> I saw three ships come sailing in
> On Christmas Day, on Christmas Day.
> I saw three ships come sailing in
> On Christmas Day in the morning.

Far below the children joined in, with their faces up-turned towards the tree. High in the branches, as the bears listened to the words, they felt as if they too were part of the wonderful cargo and sailing in one of the ships across a wave-topped sea towards an unknown shore.

"Now all the parcels will be taken down and sorted in the Bishop's palace," Boots whispered, when the last carol had been sung and the service had ended. "Stay perfectly still and hold tight."

The tree swayed and shook as willing helpers lifted down the parcels. The bears were dizzy and tumbled before their box came to rest with dozens of others piled on a long trestle table indoors.

"It doesn't look like a palace," Socks whispered, as he peered through the hole in the box. "There's only coconut-matting on the floor all frayed at the edges, and

quite an ordinary gas-cooker. The policeman's house had a much better one with a glass oven door."

"This is just one of the back kitchens," said Boots. "Big Tom said that's where everything would be sorted."

All around them Mrs. Saltmarsh and her helpers unpacked the parcels, and the bears could plainly hear their excited comments.

"Do look at these lovely bunnies, Mrs. Saltmarsh."

"And this baby doll with everything hand-knitted. It's simply charming."

"Some little chap will love this cowboy suit, and just look at these lovely scarves, all with mittens to match. Everyone has been most generous."

The bears could hardly wait for their turn.

"The cats were right. There hasn't been a single bear unpacked yet," whispered Boots. "Wait till they see us!"

At last a hand grasped their box, and someone cut the string.

"Ah, that package will be the bedroom slippers Mr. Wade promised us," said Mrs. Saltmarsh. "I want them specially for some families down by the railway. Bring them over at once, Daphne, and we'll put them aside."

A girl took off the cover and drew back the tissue paper.

"It's not bedroom slippers at all," she said, looking up with surprise, "but just three very old teddy bears."

Mrs. Saltmarsh strode across the kitchen and stared at the bears lying on the table before her. Socks's ear was still unstitched, and the canvas showed through his thin fur; Slippers's arms hung limp where the sawdust had leaked out over the years; and Boots badly needed a brush.

"If Mr. Wade was unable to send the slippers after all," she said with a frown, "I really think he should have let me know instead of sending us this pile of motheaten old toys. Naturally they will be quite useless, and I shall ring him up for a proper explanation directly I get home."

The bears huddled close together on the table. The cord fastening them together had come undone, and they were frightened of being separated, but as the other parcels were unpacked no one took any further notice of them. Soon the last of the gifts had been sorted and repacked. The parcels were piled in hampers in the hall, ready for delivery the next day. The kitchen was left shadowed and empty. Only the bears remained on the long trestle table. An icy wind rattled the back door, and snow feathered the windows. The terrible words by which they had been described still rang in their heads.

"It's all my fault," said Boots at last. "I ought to have known. They wouldn't want old toys like us to give away at Christmas."

Slippers touched the big bear's paw. Her voice was still spirited even though it trembled.

"We may be old," she said. "That's fair enough. But none of us is motheaten. No one had the right to call us that!"

"Will we be sent back to the shop now?" Socks asked. "Will everything be just the same as it was before?"

"We've burnt our bridges now," said Boots gloomily. "After we've made him look ridiculous, Mr. Wade may not want to take us back. Even though she didn't say much, you could tell Mrs. Saltmarsh was really annoyed, and he won't like that."

The big bear's words reminded them all of the splendid ships in the carol they had heard with such high hopes that afternoon, and for a while they were too miserable to talk any more.

"Then what do you suppose will happen to us?" Slippers asked at last, as she watched the snow pile along the window ledges and powder the bricks near the back door. "If we can't go back to the shop, where will we live?"

But for once Boots didn't know the answer.

It was dark in the kitchen when the door swung open and the light was switched on. The bears were too numbed with cold even to look up when someone strode across the room and halted by their table.

"Now what's been forgotten here?" said a kindly voice. "Upon my soul! It's three bears. Not as young as they once were, and worn with honest service, but none the worse for that."

A large hand gathered up the tumbled bears, and, looking up at last, they saw that the man regarding them so shrewdly was the Bishop himself.

The Bishop carried the bears into his study and set them down in a leather armchair by the fire. Tea was ready on a cart. The Bishop sat with his gaitered legs crossed and eyed the bears over the rim of a large teacup decorated with flowers and flying birds.

"Now I've seen you all somewhere, but I'm blessed if I can remember where," he remarked to himself. As he selected a crumpet from the dish, his eyes wandered around the room. The firelight shone on the vase he had won on his outing to the seaside, and as his eyes rested on it he beamed at Socks.

"Of course. You're the ginger bear Mr. Shoehorn won when we competed together at the shooting-gallery. Now I think of it, I should have known you all anywhere. You're the bears he always had in his shop. No doubt that new manager sent you away by mistake. However, no harm's done. I'll see you safe back to-morrow. In the meantime we must make you welcome, and I think I know the very best person who can do that."

The Bishop talked to the bears just as Mr. Shoehorn had always done. After tea he carried them all upstairs. In the old house they forgot they were no longer new. Everything around them was polished and well worn. Along the corridors the velvet curtains were faded like roses ready to fall, and the Persian rugs were woven in deep colors which made the bears think of jungles with tigers' eyes flashing from the darkness.

The Bishop took the bears into his dressing room.

"Now," he told them with a smile, "you shall meet one of my oldest and dearest friends."

The bears looked around the room, but no one was in sight. While they watched, the Bishop strode to a highboy and opened the top drawer. At the back of the drawer, behind the neatly piled socks and gaiters, the bears saw one of the oldest teddy bears they had ever seen. The bear's fur was the color of thick honey, his arms hung limp and empty of straw, one hind-leg was missing, so that only the swivel disc remained, and his nose was mended with black darning-wool.

"This is Mr. Chesterfield," said the Bishop, holding the old bear carefully in his arms. "While I'm busy to-night I know he'll look after you all admirably."

He set the bear among them in a wing armchair and hurried away.

The shoe shop bears never forgot the night they spent in the palace with the Bishop's bear. The old bear listened carefully to all their troubles with his head sunk forward and his boot-button eyes fixed on their faces. When they had finished he didn't try to cheer them by

denying they were old and worn; instead he told them his own story, and how he had first come to meet the Bishop.

"Rising seven he would have been when I came," he told the bears, "and as timid a little chap as you could find. Lost he looked, and scared of his own shadow. His parents were missionaries in India, and they'd left him with an aunt here in England. She was kind enough, but the house was gloomy, with stairs that creaked, and no more than gaslights on the upper landings. Soon after his parents went he caught measles. Afterwards he didn't pick up and just pecked at his food like a sparrow. No one knew what was best to be done. Iron tonics he had, and a week at Brighton, but nothing was any use. It was the cook-general who thought of a bear and bought me for him from her own wages, which weren't too large in those days, I can tell you. Bears were expensive then, and a novelty from America. We took our name of 'Teddy' from President Theodore Roosevelt himself. But I had been left in the toy-shop window too long, and the sun had taken the color from my fur in a stripe down one side, so I was sold at cost-price." The old bear glanced at the others to make sure they understood.

"Like sandals at the end of the season," said Slippers, "or a line that's gone out of fashion."

Mr. Chesterfield nodded and went on.

"Directly the boy saw me we took to one another. I'd worried about that stripe, but—bless you—he didn't care, and, without setting myself up, I think I gave the boy what he lacked. No nightlights we had, even on the first night. 'They might keep Mr. Chesterfield awake,' he told them. Kind he was, even then, with real thought for others. Of course we've had our troubles, and sometimes it's been hard, but from that first day together I don't think we've ever looked back."

Mr. Chesterfield didn't look at the bears when he spoke again. It was as if, with his head nodding on his worn chest, he dreamt of all the long, happy years he had spent with the boy who was now a man.

"You'll find there's always someone who needs you," he said, looking up at last. "It's not good looks or being young that matters, but what you can offer from your heart. A bear's job is just to be there, ready to receive all the affection that's offered, and to give it."

The bears were cheered and comforted by Mr. Chesterfield's story. If he had found a home in which to serve so well and faithfully, whatever had happened, they might yet do so too. They fell asleep at last together in the wing armchair with the moonlight shining on their golden fur, and the Bishop's frogged dressing-gown thrown over them to keep out the cold.

Bears for Christmas

"YOUR MIND simply isn't on your work these days," Mr. Wade told Polly the moment she entered the shop the next day. "This affair with the Christmas tree has made me the laughing-stock of the whole town. The thought of those bears being unpacked in public appalls me, particularly as the press was present and they were noted down as the contribution from this shop. Mrs. Saltmarsh was quite rightly disappointed and shocked. How you could have made such a ridiculous mistake I shall never understand."

"But I did pack the slippers in the box," Polly protested. "I didn't even know the bears weren't still in the shop. There was so much to do I hadn't time to notice, and the moment we shut I had to hurry home to get the children their tea."

"That's exactly what I complain of," said her employer. "Each day you arrive late and by half-past five you always have one eye on the clock."

"I know, sir, and I'm sorry," said Polly with a sob,

83

"but there's so much to do at home before I leave, and more waiting when I get back."

Mr. Wade coughed, and rubbed a pair of evening-pumps hard with a yellow duster. Polly certainly looked tired, but if she had too much work to do at home it was really no business of his.

"Now, tears won't mend matters," he said shortly. "How this unfortunate affair occurred we may never know. The best thing we can do now is to set it right. I want you to find the missing slippers immediately and take them straight along to the palace; then they will be just in time to be dispatched with the other gifts."

Polly found the slippers at last, hidden at the back of the stockroom.

"They were right under the boxes of last year's sandals," she told the manager, "but I am sure I never put them there. What would have been the point?"

Mr. Wade sniffed. He disliked being asked questions, especially when he was still so upset.

"Never mind that now," he told her. "Pack them up at once. This time I shall fasten the box myself to make sure there are no further mistakes."

Polly packed the slippers while Mr. Wade watched, as if at any moment he expected the slippers to skip from the box and disappear.

When the parcel was ready Polly hesitated by the shop door with the box in her arms. Mr. Wade still looked forbidding. He was on the telephone, talking to the local reporter, to make sure details of his shop's gift were corrected before they appeared in print.

"Well, what is it now?" he asked, as he finished his call.

"I wanted to know if I should ask for the bears and bring them back," said Polly. "Will they still be at the palace?"

"I don't know, and I'm sure I don't care," said Mr. Wade testily. "Do just as you choose. As far as I am concerned, I shall be perfectly happy if I never clap eyes on those creatures again."

The conversation he had had with Mrs. Saltmarsh the day before was still vivid in his mind. Her words, though restrained and polite, had stung like salt on a cut finger. He had done his best to explain that a mistake had occurred, and he thought that she had understood. To make doubly sure, and as a token of his good intentions, he had included in the parcel half a dozen pairs of their best angora bedsocks. Even at cost-price the extra donation would be a considerable expense, and one he would have to meet entirely from his own pocket.

The Bishop's Rolls-Royce stopped outside the shoe shop half an hour later. It was very old, and the yellow coach-work gleamed in the snowy street like the sun itself. The Bishop was in the back seat. Beside him sat Polly Trinket, with the shoe shop bears on her lap.

"Your young assistant has explained everything admirably," the Bishop told Mr. Wade as he ushered him into the shop. "Mrs. Saltmarsh, who has organized our scheme so well, was delighted with your most generous gift. She asked me to tell you she quite appreciates how the little mistake occurred at such a busy season as this. I was just setting out with the bears, to return them to you, when this young lady arrived, so we've traveled together."

"My lord, you really shouldn't have troubled to bring the bears back," said Mr. Wade. "They're quite worn out. For some time now I had decided to replace them with a tank of tropical fish. Children nowadays like something far more up to date than a few grubby stuffed toys."

The Bishop hesitated in the shop doorway.

"Of course you know your own business best," he said, "and must do as you think fit, but for my part I think children don't change much down the years. What comforted us when we were young comforts them just as well."

The Bishop hurried back to his car without another word. Standing on the shop step, Mr. Wade's eyes were riveted, not on the Bishop, but on an elderly bear perched on the seat at his side. Snow blew in the shop-keeper's face, but Mr. Wade only blinked and continued to stare. As the car glided forward he could have sworn that the Bishop bent down towards the bear and spoke earnestly to him, as he might have shared some confidence with a very old friend.

When he re-entered the shop Mr. Wade still looked pale and shaken. Polly was brushing the bears, and he spoke more sharply to her than he really intended.

"Put those bears away in the stockroom at once. They had better go for the time being in the hamper with the other remnants. I can't have them littering up the shop any longer."

With the bears in her arms, Polly hesitated. She spoke

at last, with her back to the manager, and the red hair tumbling across her bent face.

"Please, sir, if you really don't want the bears any more might I . . ."

Mr. Wade didn't hear her unfinished request. Glancing up from his accounts, he only saw her still in the shop.

"Now this is no time to dawdle," he said. "For goodness' sake make haste. We've wasted half the morning as it is. Put those bears away, and let us proceed with our proper work."

The bears lay tumbled in the hamper in the stockroom.

"Don't worry, I'll look after you," Polly had whispered before leaving them, but none of them could see how.

During the lunch hour Polly didn't go out. She sat knitting as if her whole life depended on every stitch. She didn't stop even to speak to the bears.

"I expect it's Christmas presents," said Socks. Then he wished he hadn't, for none of them wanted to think about Christmas or presents just then. They sat staring at a pair of Louis-heeled silver shoes which had been in every sale for as long as they could remember, a plastic sandal with a missing buckle, and a single left-footed gum boot. What had happened to the other boot no one had ever discovered. The bears knew very well that quite a number of the articles now surrounding them would one day be thrown into the trash-can.

The shop was crowded all that afternoon. Everyone was buying last-minute presents. Even Mr. Wade looked pleased. At teatime the telephone rang, and a few minutes later he called for Polly.

"The dancing troupe in the pantomime that's opening on Boxing Day want some ballet shoes in a hurry," he told her. "Their luggage has been held up by the snow. I told them it was rather late, but if you could run along to the theater with what we have I should be most obliged."

"Of course I will," said Polly.

The manager thought Polly looked tired as she left the shop with the shoe boxes tucked under her arm. At the last moment he hurried to the door and called after her, "Don't worry about coming back. Go straight home. I'll shut up the shop."

But Polly, hurrying down the street with her ears muffled against the cold, never heard his parting instructions.

At five o'clock Mr. Wade turned the notice on the door to CLOSED, locked up the shop, and left for home.

The shop was silent, and in the hamper the bears shivered with cold.

"There's nothing Polly can do for us now," said Socks. "Mr. Wade has padlocked the door and gone off with the key."

"If Polly promised she would do something she'll try," said Boots stoutly. "All we have to do is wait."

The snowflakes were cool on Polly's glowing face as she ran back towards the shop with her errand done. All day she had tried to muster up enough courage to ask Mr. Wade once more about the bears. Now she was determined to do so. Of course he'll say "yes," she told herself. When he knows why I need them he'll understand. As she turned down Cordwainer's Row, Polly knew exactly what she must say. On this night of all nights, no one would refuse. Mr. Wade was often worried and impatient, but deep down he was as kind as anyone else. For the sake of the bears and the happiness of those she loved best, Polly was determined to speak.

When she saw the shop in darkness, it was as if the light was switched off in her own eyes. The CLOSED sign swung on its cord, and the door was padlocked. Polly pressed her nose to the glass, but in the shop nothing stirred. The boxes were white in the gloom, and the fitting-stools were ranged neatly in rows.

Polly turned sadly away. Tears prickled her eyes as she went home. In her pocket, wrapped in tissue paper, was a yellow scarf, a royal blue jumper with pearl buttons, and a green tam-o'-shanter hat with a red bobble, all made to fit the three bears now lying discarded and unwanted in the padlocked shop.

The bears were asleep when the noise woke them. Outside the town was silent. Footsteps were muffled on the snowy pavements. Only the cathedral clock chimed the hours.

"There's someone trying to open the skylight in the cloakroom," whispered Boots.

"Perhaps it's Hobson or the cathedral cats," suggested Slippers.

"Not tonight," whispered Boots. "The bacon-counter man took Hobson home in a New Zealand butter box, and the others would be in the cathedral. It's nearly time for the Midnight Service."

"Then it's burglars," said Socks.

They thought of the feathered slippers from Paris, the evening shoes with jeweled heels, the shoe buckles set with brilliants, the collection-box for the Fabric Fund, and the toffee-tin, with an Alsatian on the lid, full of stamps, paper fasteners, and pins. They forgot all Mr. Wade had ever said about their being out of date and in the way. They only knew it was their duty to defend the shop, and, as bears, none of them was afraid.

"We'll have to give an alarm," said Boots.

"But how?" asked Slippers.

"On the telephone," whispered Socks. "It's lucky it's in here. You dial 999. That brings the police, the ambulance, and the fire-brigade."

"We don't really need a fire-engine," said Slippers doubtfully, "or an ambulance yet."

"You needn't have them all," said Boots. "You tell them which."

"But how can we?" objected Slippers. "No one would expect us to talk."

While the bears hesitated half-way to the telephone, the skylight creaked open. Someone dropped lightly to the floor and ran across the shop. Before the bears could move, the door of the stockroom swung open, and Polly Trinket gathered them into her arms.

"I told you that I would look after you," she said, with a sob. "Now I've come to take you all home."

As she spoke, a key turned in the padlock on the shop door, and over Polly's shoulder the bears saw the tall figure of Mr. Wade himself.

"And what, may I ask, is the meaning of this?" he

asked, staring at Polly with the bears in her arms. "I was on my way to the service at the cathedral when I noticed a light and decided to investigate it."

Polly stood before the manager in a dusty pair of tartan trousers and a torn duffle coat.

"I climbed in through the skylight to get the bears," she said. "I wanted to ask you if I might have them all day, only this morning you were too cross to listen, and when I came back from delivering the shoes the shop was shut. I knew you meant to throw them away, and I didn't think it would matter if I took the bears first and told you after."

The manager shook the snow from his umbrella and sat down on one of the fitting-stools. He took his shoehorn from his pocket, as if just holding it in his hand made him feel less bewildered.

"But why did you want the bears so much you had to break into my shop to get them?" he asked.

"I needed them for Bill and Audrey and Simon," said Polly. "They're my brothers and sister. I'd thought and thought what to give them for Christmas, and when you said you didn't want the bears in the shop any more I knew they were just what I had been trying to find. I've knitted them all something new to wear, only none of the clothes would have been any use without the bears to wear them."

Polly took the jumper, scarf, and hat from her pocket, and spread them on her knee. She was crying so much the tears spilled on the brightly colored wool, and in silence Mr. Wade handed her a double-strength paper handkerchief.

91

"Since Father died Mum and I have always managed to take care of the others," Polly went on. "Then this winter she was ill. She's been in hospital three weeks now, and I've had to do as best I can alone. Mum worried about us having a real Christmas, and I told her I'd fix everything. There's a pudding made, and a cake, and a frozen chicken, but after everything was paid for there wasn't anything left for presents, and I didn't want the others to have none at all. Only now if I'm sent to prison there won't be anyone to look after the others, and just when Mum's so much better, it will break her heart."

Mr. Wade polished his spectacles and blew his nose. He looked at the bears as if he had never seen them properly before. Without speaking, he took the yellow scarf and knotted it around Slippers's neck. He dressed Boots in the blue jumper and adjusted the tam-o'-shanter on the smallest bear's head.

"Now," he said, "I think you had better all come home with me. This is a matter my wife can deal with far better than me, and we'll see what she thinks should be done."

The bears and Polly had never thought of Mr. Wade being married or living in a house at all, with chimneys and a trash-can and rosebushes in the flower-beds.

Mrs. Wade was large and comfortable. Even her hair-curlers were different colors. The small house seemed to overflow with Christmas cheer. Directly the front door was opened they smelled mince pies, and Christmas cards were piled on every shelf and table.

"What's best to be done is for this young woman to

have a good night's sleep," declared Mrs. Wade, after she had listened to the whole tale. "As for the bears, they must go home with Polly. Under the circumstances she couldn't have thought of anything better for her brothers and little sister."

She gave Polly a hot drink and a bunch of chrysanthemums straight from a cut-glass vase on the upright piano to take to her mother the next day. Afterwards she and Mr. Wade saw Polly and the bears to her door.

The bears were very sleepy when they reached the small terraced house in which they were to live. A bunch of holly hung on the door, and the step was stoned snow-white. The narrow hall was hung with hand-made paper-chains, and sprigs of holly stuck behind the pictures prickled the bears' fur as they were carried upstairs.

Socks sat at the foot of Audrey's bed, while Boots and Slippers sat at the foot of Bill's and Simon's. In the moonlight they could just see the faces of the sleeping children, full of expectant happiness because tomorrow was Christmas Day.

"The Bishop's bear was perfectly right," whispered Slippers. "There's always someone who needs a bear, and whether you're old or new just doesn't matter."

It was the happiest Christmas the bears had ever had, and better than all their dreams. At lunch the bears sat around the table, and the children served them Brussels sprouts and raisins. There was even wine made from cochineal in glass egg-cups. Boots wore his new jersey, Slippers her scarf, and Socks his cap, even though it was indoors.

After lunch Polly took the children and the bears to see her mother in hospital. Mrs. Trinket was so much better, she told them she was coming home at the end of the week.

"You're a good girl, Polly," she told her, as she admired the bears. "You've managed everything." And, meeting her eyes, Polly knew her mother guessed just how hard presents for them all had been to find.

Going home, they all felt tired. The bears lolled against the children's coats, and Polly yawned. She thought they had better have boiled eggs for supper to save the chicken.

She was setting the supper table when a knock sounded on the door. The children ran to open it. On the step, stamping their feet in the cold, stood Mr. Wade and the Bishop. From the Bishop's pocket Mr. Chesterfield peered out, and in the Bishop's arms was a hamper.

"Mr. Wade has told me all that has happened," said the Bishop, "and, if you won't take it amiss, we've brought you all some presents from the Christmas tree."

Mr. Wade and the Bishop helped them unpack the hamper. There were crackers from Hobson's shop, the cake like the Yuletide log, and shoes for them all from Mr. Wade's shop—silver sandals for Polly, red leather-barred shoes for her sister, and bright-blue puddle-boots for the boys.

"And we have the bears, too," said Polly, after she and the others had thanked the Bishop and Mr. Wade for their gifts. "They were on the Christmas tree, too, and the best present of them all."

The bears saw Mr. Chesterfield for a moment alone before the grown-ups left.

"Remember us to Hobson and the other cats," Boots told him. "Tell them we've found just the home we needed."

"And they'll be welcome any time they care to call," added Slippers. "It's no more than a step."

"There's a pane missing in the wash-house window," said Socks, "so they'll easily get in."

The old bear promised to pass on all their messages.

"I'm more glad than I can say that everything has worked out so well," he said, pressing Boots's paw with his own. "You'll be loved and needed here, and that's all any bear could wish."

Standing on the steps, with the bears in their arms, the children and Polly waved as the Bishop and the shoe-shop manager drove slowly away down the street and the car's crimson tail lamps disappeared in the fast-falling snow.